4/06

The Zoo Rap

This edition first published in 2006 by
Sea-to-Sea Publications
1980 Lookout Drive
North Mankato
Minnesota 56003

Printed in China

Library of Congress Cataloging-in-Publication Data:

Clare, James.
  The zoo rap / by James Clare.
    p. cm. — (Reading corner)
  Summary: A rhyming counting book featuring a trip to the zoo.
  ISBN 1-59771-003-2
  [1. Zoos—Fiction. 2. Counting. 3. Stories in rhyme.] I. Title. II. Series.

PZ8.3.C5383Zo 2005
[E]—dc22
                                                    2004063625

9 8 7 6 5 4 3 2

Published by arrangement with the Watts Publishing Group Ltd, London

Series Editor: Jackie Hamley
Series Advisors: Linda Gambrell, Dr. Barrie Wade, Dr. Hilary Minns
Design: Peter Scoulding

The Zoo Rap

Written by
James Clare

Illustrated by
Barbara Vagnozzi

SEA-TO-SEA
Mankato Collingwood London

James Clare

"I have four children and two cats so my house is very noisy! I love writing books. I hope you enjoy this one!"

Barbara Vagnozzi

"I have two children, a dog, two cats, four ducks and two rabbits... my own little zoo!"

One, two...

5

We're going to the zoo!

Three, four...

We hear the lions roar!

10

Five, six...

We see the monkeys'
tricks!

Seven, eight...

17

It's getting very late.

19

Nine, ten...

21

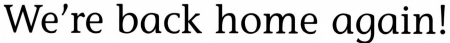

We're back home again!

23

Notes for parents and teachers

READING CORNER has been structured to provide maximum support for new readers. The stories may be used by adults for sharing with young children. Primarily, however, the stories are designed for newly independent readers, whether they are reading these books in bed at night, or in the reading corner at school or in the library.

Starting to read alone can be a daunting prospect. **READING CORNER** helps by providing visual support and repeating words and phrases, while making reading enjoyable. These books will develop confidence in the new reader, and encourage a love of reading that will last a lifetime!

If you are reading this book with a child, here are a few tips:

1. Make reading fun! Choose a time to read when you and the child are relaxed and have time to share the story.

2. Encourage children to reread the story, and to retell the story in their own words, using the illustrations to remind them what has happened.

3. Give praise! Remember that small mistakes need not always be corrected.

READING CORNER covers three grades of early reading ability, with three levels at each grade. Each level has a certain number of words per story, indicated by the number of bars on the spine of the book, to allow you to choose the right book for a young reader:

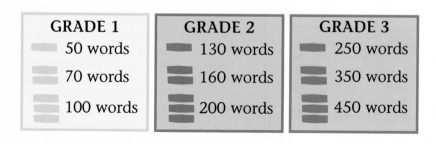

GRADE 1	GRADE 2	GRADE 3
50 words	130 words	250 words
70 words	160 words	350 words
100 words	200 words	450 words